Jessica Takes Charge

by Linda LaRose
illustrated by Leanne Franson

Annick Press Ltd.
Toronto • New York • Vancouver

Jessica knew there was a monster in the house. Her mom and dad didn't believe it.

"There's a monster in the house, guys," she told them.

"Nonsense," said Daddy.

"Very doubtful," said Mommy.

"I hear it growling at night," said Jessica.

"Piffle," said her dad.

"Rannygazoo," said her mom.

When Gramps came for dinner, Jessica told him about it.

"I'm not surprised," he said. "Did I ever tell you about the monster I found when I was a little boy?" And right then and there he told her about his monster.

Later, Jessica sat on her favourite step. She thought and thought and thought.

When she finished thinking, she said, “I’m going to find that monster myself.” Stuffed monsters lived in her room, but “I bet real monsters live in the basement,” thought Jessica. “I’ll look down there tonight, after Mommy and Daddy are asleep.”

Jessica lay in bed, waiting. Her fuzzy slippers made two big lumps under the covers.

After a very long time, Jessica peeked out her door. She went through the dark, dark hall, past Mommy’s and Dad’s bedroom.

Part way down the stairs, something touched her hand!

Jessica flicked her black pigtails so they stood out from the sides of her head. Then she remembered her balloon stuck to the ceiling. Its string had tickled her hand!

She kept going down, down, down ...

Bump! Bang! Ouch!

What was that?!?

Jessica stayed as quiet as the tiniest bug. Then she thought of the trap she'd made for catching monsters. The trap had caught *her*!

"Wish I had a flashlight," thought Jessica.

Tiptoeing wasn't easy in her fuzzy slippers. But she tiptoed the rest of the way to the Basement Door!

The door sque-e-eaked open. She took a big step ... right onto something oozy-squishy that went "ssppfftt."

Jessica threw herself at the light switch. It was the wet sponge! She'd used it to wash her green fingerprints from the door earlier.

The last place to check was the workshop. Jessica went to the door. She swung it open.

The workshop looked darker than the deepest, darkest hole. The light switch was in the middle of the room. Should she go in and turn on the light?

No! Instead, she ran at top-notch speed. She didn't stop running until she stood on the top basement step.

The first thing Jessica heard when she stopped was—growling! It wasn't Muesli growling, because the sound was coming from upstairs. But maybe Muesli could help.

"Come, Muesli," she said, but he whimpered from behind the sofa. That's where he always hid at night. That's where he stayed now. "Bad dog, Muesli," hissed Jessica.

Then Jessica saw just what she needed. Beside the drippy-wet sponge was her sand pail. It was still full of nice cold water.

Jessica picked up the pail and went upstairs. Water slopped out of the pail as it bumped against her leg.

The farther up she went, the louder the growly sound got. It was coming from Mommy's and Daddy's bedroom!

Jessica pushed open their door.

Where had the monster gone? It sounded like it had crawled into bed beside Daddy.

Jessica sneaked over to his side. She threw back the covers and splashed the monster with the cold water!

There were two sharp yelps. Then the light on Mommy's side flashed on.

Mommy sat blinking, Daddy dripping.

"What the ...!" spluttered Daddy.

"Jessica Jones!" exclaimed Mommy. "What are you doing?!?"

"I'm catching that monster," said Jessica.

"There *is* no monster!"

"I heard it growling right here," said Jessica, flicking her left pigtail.

"That was your dad snoring!"

"Snorting?"

"Snoring! And those stuffed monsters of yours are going to be put away !" said Mommy.

"Why?" asked Jessica.

"Because they give you bad ideas," said Daddy. "And so does Gramps."

"Where will they be put?"

"In the spare room."

"Will Gramps be put away too?" Jessica asked.

"I'll have a word with Gramps tomorrow," said Daddy.

Jessica was *very* helpful cleaning up the big mess. She patted Daddy's wet hair with his sock. She carried stuffed monsters to the spare-room closet and soggy sheets to the laundry-room basket.

Finally, she was back in bed. The covers were tucked tight under her chin. Two good-night kisses tingled on her cheek.

At the other end of the hall, Mommy and Daddy laughed. Jessica smiled.

Looking for a real monster was hard work. She hugged her fuzzy slippers closer and nestled deeper into the covers. She remembered green paint on Muesli's tail. Tomorrow she'd give it a good wash in the bathroom.

The last drop of water slid from the sand pail into the carpet by her bed. Way down the hall she could hear Daddy. He was snorting himself to sleep.

Jessica fell asleep too.

Cover design: Sheryl Shapiro

We acknowledge the support of the Canada Council for the Arts for our publishing program. We also thank the Ontario Arts Council.

Cataloguing in Publication Data
LaRose, Linda
Jessica takes charge

ISBN 1-55037-563-6 (bound) ISBN 1-55037-562-8 (pbk.)

I. Franson, Leanne. II. Title.

PS8572.A76J47 1999 jC813'.54 C98-932135-5
PZ7.L37Je 1999

The art in this book was rendered in water-colours.
The text was typeset in Cheltenham.

Distributed in Canada by:
Firefly Books Ltd.
3680 Victoria Park Avenue
Willowdale, ON
M2H 3K1

Published in the U.S.A. by Annick Press (U.S.) Ltd.
Distributed in the U.S.A. by:
Firefly Books (U.S.) Inc.
P.O. Box 1338
Ellicott Station
Buffalo, NY 14205

Printed and bound in Canada by
Friesens, Altona, Manitoba

Linda LaRose

To Christopher

Leanne Franson

For Mues'i–
Good doggy, with love!